little Sir Galahad

BY

LILLIAN HOLMES

REWRITTEN BY MARK HAMBY

LAMPLIGHTER
Publishing
BUILDING CHRISTIAN CHARACTER ... ONE HEART AT A TIME

Little Sir Galahad.
Copyright © 2003 by Mark Hamby
All rights reserved.
First Printing, September 2003
Thirteenth Printing, August 2020

Published by Lamplighter Publishing; a division of Lamplighter
Ministries International.

Printed at the Lamplighter Bindery, Mount Morris, NY.

The Lamplighter Collection is a collection of Christian family literature
from the 17th, 18th and 19th centuries. Each edition is printed in an
attractive hard-bound collector's format. For more information, call us at
1-888-A-GOSPEL (1-888-246-7735) or 1-570-585-1314, visit us at *www.
lamplighter.net* or write:

> Lamplighter Publishing
> 23 State Street
> Mount Morris, NY 14510

Author: Lillian Holmes
Executive Editor: Mark Hamby
Chief Editor: Deborah Hamby
Historical Research: Darlene Catlett
Copy Editors: Darlene Catlett, Deborah Hamby, Shelly Curry
Cover Design: Michal Rudolph

ISBN: 1-58474-100-7
ISBN-13: 978-1-58474-100-8
Blue Ribbon, K900, S23-RL

Preface.

Since the "sad thing" happened, young David spends his days sitting beside his window, watching the children and working people of Alverton pass by. He is so rich in sunny smiles and imaginative play that they have no reason to call him "poor David." His greatest desire is to become strong again, but David learns that real strength comes in fighting his own temper and choosing to do what is right, especially when it is so difficult!

Because of his pure heart, inner strength, and noble deeds, David is donned "Sir Galahad," an honorable title for one "whose strength is as the strength of ten because his heart is pure."

When I first came upon this little book, I knew I had stumbled upon a work that would serve as a model to help young boys and girls overcome the temptation to treat weaker children with ill will. I believe you will find *Little Sir Galahad* to be one of our best Lamplighter stories for children, and, as always, for adults as well.

Mark Hamby
Matthew 5

Publisher's note: The rules of punctuation, spelling, and even sentence structure of the 1800s were different than our present-day standards. We have chosen to keep the original format as much as possible, editing only when deemed necessary.

LITTLE SIR GALAHAD.

LITTLE SIR GALAHAD.

CHAPTER I.

LOOKING OUT THE WINDOW.

is real name was David — a beautiful name, and one that he himself liked, because it had belonged to the Bible boy to whom such wonderful things happened.

"Read about David," he used to say to Aunt Jane when it was time for their evening chapter; and he never grew tired of hearing about the ruddy, vigorous boy who had killed a lion and a bear, and even a giant.

"I want to be like that David," he began to tell Aunt Jane almost as soon as he could talk plainly; and by being like him he meant being very strong. When he was only five years old, he came in one evening in great glee, crying out, "I'm strong! I can carry more wood than a boy that's seven!"

He never heard of Galahad until after the sad thing happened which made him think he could no longer hope to be like David. He would never have heard of him at all, if it had not been for Arthur Bryan. It seemed as if all the pleasantness came into his life through Arthur after that, just as all the sunshine came to him through the little window that looked toward Arthur's home on the hill across the river. The sun did not come around to it until afternoon for it was a west window, but David felt better in the mornings, and did not need so much to be enlivened then; so he was thankful the window was on that side of the house. It was toward the mill yard, too, so that the people went right under it as they passed back and forth to their work; and that was pleasant, for David had many friends among the "hands," as he called them.

You strong boys who scarcely know which way your window faces wonder why all this was of consequence. Well, at the time, David was a cripple, and could not move more than a few yards from his window without tiring himself very much. He had spent nearly all the days since he was five years old at that place, and now he was almost eight.

At first folks said as they passed, "Poor boy! It's a pity the Lord did not take him to his mother!" But the Lord always leaves people as long as He has work for them, and He often has things for a lame boy to do. After awhile the people forgot to say this. David was so rich in sunny smiles, they could not call him poor.

God had taken his mother home when he was just learning to walk. He was a strong, sturdy little fellow then, with large, thoughtful blue eyes and jet black hair. His father worked on the railroad, and was home for only a night now and then; so when David no longer had his mother, he had to be taken to Alverton, the little factory town where his father's sister lived and worked. There did not seem to be any place for him there, for Aunt Jane could not give him much care. She worked in the factory from half-past five in the afternoon, and she did not know anything about children anyhow.

But there was no other place for David. Nobody knew anything about his mother's people except that she had displeased them when she married David's father.

Next door to Aunt Jane there was a woman who had four children, and she promised to look after David all she could while Aunt Jane was away every day. That was easier than you might think, for in Shop Row the houses were very close together; indeed it was all one big house, for it had once been an old store-house belonging to the factories, and had afterward been divided into tenements,[1] the whole ten of which were no larger than Arthur's home. Some of them had doors opening into each other,

---

[1] Apartments or rooms for rent.

and Aunt Jane's communicated with Mrs. Black's in that way. Most of the time David was in Mrs. Black's house, or, if she wanted all the children out of the way, she sent the five into Aunt Jane's.

David was a very obedient boy almost always. He felt as if he did not belong anywhere, and he seemed to be trying to make as little trouble as possible. Although he enjoyed romping games, it was very seldom anyone was hurt in them.

As he grew older he liked to play stories best. He did not know any stories except those Aunt Jane told him in the evenings, and she knew only Bible stories. Mrs. Black's children never heard any except those he told them, so they played selling Joseph into Egypt, finding Moses in his little boat, making bricks out of mud, without straw, or—what David liked best of all—killing Goliath with a stone. A big tree trunk across the road from Shop Row was Goliath. It had to be laboriously hauled to an upright position, and as it did not fall down when hit with the stone, somebody had to knock it over.

Sometimes Alice Black wanted to be David, and her own brother very contemptuously told her, "A girl can't be! Girls don't know how to throw straight!"

But David would say kindly, "Maybe they could in those days. It was a long while ago when Goliath was killed."

So Alice would slay the giant in her turn.

I do not know where David learned to be so kind to girls and women. I suppose he had never quenched that instinct of chivalry[2] with which every boy must be endowed,[3] in a greater or lesser degree. He saw the men around him let their wives carry heavy buckets of water from the spring while they lounged at the doors of their houses. Some of them even let their wives and children earn a living for them, but David seemed to know he must not follow in their steps. He was

---

[2] The ideal qualifications of a knight, including courtesy, generosity, bravery, honor, and gallantry.
[3] Provided with by his Creator.

always telling Aunt Jane he would soon be big enough to go to the factory and earn money for them both, so that she need not work any more.

The day the sad thing happened he had been protesting because the boys wanted to make the girls drag the sleds up the hill before they would let them have a ride.

"I'll pull your sled up twice, if you'll let me come down once," Alice Black had just said.

"I'm lots stronger than you," he replied. "I'll pull you up on it, and then we'll both come down together."

"I'M LOTS STRONGER THAN YOU," DAVID REPLIED.

The other boys laughed at him for being so silly, and he had turned around to shout something to them. I think he was going to say, "You're not strong enough to pull a girl up the hill!" I am afraid he was too vain[4] of his strength. He did not say it, though, for Alice began to scream as they started off down the hill; and before he quite knew what was the matter, she had rolled off, and he and the sled were mixed up with the horses of a big sleigh which had been coming along the road at the foot of the hill, and which he had not seen or heard, because he was thinking about the boys. The man pulled up his horses immediately, but not before David had been kicked in the back, and—the sad thing had happened.

---

[4] Excessively proud.

CHAPTER II.

"Jesus Is My Bruther."

t was nearly three years since that happening now, and all the time David had been thinking he would be well after awhile; but although he could sometimes walk across the room, he had never been able to go even as far as the tree-trunk, Goliath, and most of the time he had to stay in the chair at the window.

When David saw Alice and George Black start off to school, how he longed to be with them! Alice tried to teach him all she was learning, and soon he could read as well as she; but that was not very well, after all.

He asked Aunt Jane all the hard

words in the Bible chapters about David, and he could read them for himself after a time; but at last he almost gave up the hope of being like that David. No matter how often Aunt Jane reminded him that it was the Lord's strength that helped David, our wounded little David replied, "Yes, but he wasn't lame."

But from this you must not think that he was gloomy. There were few brighter, happier boys anywhere. He had the slate[5] and Reader[6] that the teacher of the village school had sent him, and he drew strange animals, or read over and over the stories in the Reader.

Then there were all his friends to make him happy. This was before he knew Arthur, but he had a great many friends even then, and he liked to think that over. Sometimes he counted them over to Aunt Jane.

"First, there's Mr. Stanton," he would say. "I used to be afraid of him. But he's very nice. He laughs to me every time he goes past, and you know he gave me a

---

[5] A small writing surface made of rock.
[6] A textbook for instruction and practice in reading.

kite to fly out of the window. And there's Sarah Watson, too. She's the cook up at the superintendent's house, you know. Nearly every time she passes on her way to the store, she comes in for a minute. And Mike makes three; he drives the wagon, you know. There are about ten altogether."

"How did you get acquainted with Mike?" Aunt Jane asked.

"One day he dropped some wood out of the wagon, and he didn't know, so I called to him. After he put it in, he came and talked to me. Now he always says, 'Good-mornin' to you,' or, 'How are ye today?' He has a little brother about as big as me."

That night after the chapter had been read, David said, "I have another friend, too."

"A new one?" Aunt Jane inquired.

"It's God," David replied earnestly. "I was thinking today that I wished I had a father or else a big brother, and then I remembered 'Our Father.'"

"Yes," Aunt Jane replied, "God is the

best Father."

"And I have a big brother, too," David continued.

Aunt Jane was silent, waiting for him to explain, as she knew he would.

"If God is my Father, Jesus is my Brother. I was talking to Mr. Stanton about it this evening. He stopped at the window when he was going home from the mill. I said it would be nice to have a big brother like Mike."

"Mike would have to go away from you all day," Aunt Jane remarked.

"Yes, I know. I 'membered that afterward. Then Mr. Stanton said we all had an Elder Brother who could be with us all the time. Right away I knew what he meant. I always know what Mr. Stanton means. When I was little and went to prayer-meetings with you, before—you know—" and his voice trembled a little— "I never could tell what any of 'em talked about, 'cept Mr. Stanton. Once he told about the Good S'maritan and 'splained how we could be like him." Then, more slowly: "Aunt

Jane, if Jesus is my Brother, why don't he make me well?"

"Do you think Mr. Stanton asked that when he sprained his ankle?" replied Aunt Jane. "He just tried to bear it bravely."

"He told me 'bout it one day," David replied. "He said God wanted him to think, he s'posed. He had never kept quiet long before, and had not thought about him enough. He said he learned a good many things then."

"Maybe your Elder Brother wants you to think," suggested Aunt Jane.

"I s'pect he does; I ought to have known it. I never knew he was my Friend, and I never knew I had so many friends until I had to be alone so much."

The next day David washed one side of his slate very carefully, and wrote at the top: "Things I am—." He wanted to put "learning," but he did not know how to spell it. He waited until Sarah Watson came along to ask her, but she wasn't very sure. She thought it was "lerning," however; so he wrote it that way. Then very laboriously he put underneath it:

> God wants me to lern about
> him. He is my friend.
> Jesus is my bruther.
> He is the best kind of a
> bruther, bekaws he can stay
> with you always.

He was not sure of the spelling of other words than "learning," but he concluded it would not be worthwhile to ask Mike. He thought he would let Mr. Stanton correct the spelling some day when he had time to wait a few minutes.

Several days passed before anything more went down; and then one afternoon Alice Black exclaimed, as she watched him write something she was dictating, "You write a great deal better than I do, David! It's because you have so much time to write. I wish I had time to write at home."

He thought a long while about it when she had gone home. There were some pleasant things he had that strong boys and girls did not have. After a while he added to his list:

If God makes you keep still, he gives you things to make up.

There were days and days when it rained that March. Nothing happened. The people who usually smiled at him seemed scarcely to have time to remember him as they hurried past the window. The rain dripped through the cracks around the doors; Shop Row looked very dreary. But after awhile the sun shone again, and then Arthur came.

Arthur's father was a doctor, and lived in the big house on the hill across the river from Alverton. Arthur went to school in Elkton, the town on the other side of the hills, but sometimes he walked over to Alverton with his father. A big collie dog usually accompanied him, and David loved to watch for him. He had never seen so fine a dog before.

This special day in March, after all

the rain, Arthur and Sancho both felt particularly frisky because they had been kept in the house so long. They ran races down the hill, across the bridge, and up the road that passes Shop Row.

HE THOUGHT A LONG WHILE ABOUT IT.

CHAPTER III.

unt Jane's gray cat was in the house, curled up against the door, asleep. There was a crack under the door—quite a big one—that let in rain and snow sometimes; and if she had not been a very foolish cat she would not have lain right against it, so that the end of her tail and some of her fur stuck out to entice Sancho to attack. How could any dog resist such a temptation? He sniffed at Tabby, and when she drew herself away from the door, he threw his whole weight against it, and came bounding in. Tabby spit at him, and behaved most impolitely to her guest;

but the guest was impolite, too, for he began to chase her around the room. Chairs fell down, the carpet was rolled up wherever it could be — it seemed as if a live whirlwind was in the house!

David laughed and laughed. He was sorry for poor Tabby, too; but then, he was sure Sancho would not hurt her because he had watched him chase cats before. He called to his pet, and when at last she sprang to his window, he seized her in his arms and ordered Sancho to be quiet.

Another laugh joined his, and, looking up, he saw Arthur at the door.

"Sancho! Sancho!" Arthur called. Then to David, "Oh, wasn't it funny? Did he hurt anything?"

"No," David answered, as soon as he could stop laughing, "he only upset everything."

"Let's fix it all straight again," Arthur said; but suddenly pausing, he added, "Are you the lame boy father told me about?"

"I am lame," David said. "You're the

boy up at the big house on the hill. I see you up there with your dog."

"Yes, my name's Arthur Bryan. What's yours?"

"David Grandon."

Arthur busied himself picking up the chairs and smoothing the carpet, chatting all the while about Sancho and his other dog, which his father would not often let him bring out.

"He's big, but he's young," he said. "I believe you could ride on him, though, and then we could play tournament. I have to play alone nearly always, and that makes you have to make-believe too much."

"How do you play that?" asked David.

"I play I'm King Arthur. Sometimes I get on Sancho's back, if he'll let me. King Arthur had lots of knights—men who fought on horseback—and they called the fights tournaments."

"Is he in the Bible? Aunt Jane never reads about him."

"No, he is in another book I have.

Your king is in the Bible — King David!
You can play king, too."

"I can't be that now. He wasn't lame;
he was strong."

"Yes, I know; but s'pose he had been
lame. Make believe he was."

"He would have to just keep still like
I do."

At this point Dr. Bryan appeared
in search of Arthur, and when he saw
Sancho at the door of Aunt Jane's house,
he looked in and was glad to find Arthur
talking to David.

"How are you today, my man?" he
asked David.

"Pretty well, thank you," David
replied.

The doctor asked him some questions
about his back, and said, half to himself,
"It seems as if that ought to get well."

When he and Arthur departed, they
promised that Arthur should come again,
and Arthur added, "I'll bring the book
that tells about the tournaments. There's
more in it than the fighting. Mamma
says if I play King Arthur, I must be a

Christian knight. That's why I wear this little blue ribbon. She put it there to help me not to forget the King that was King Arthur's King, too. You know about Him, don't you?" David nodded.

He had so much to think about that afternoon that it did not seem long until half-past five. He stroked Tabby gently and said, "Oh, you nice old cat! If you hadn't put your tail under the door, Sancho wouldn't have upset everything, and Arthur wouldn't have come in. I won't call you silly any more."

He told Aunt Jane all about his visitor, and when he prayed that night, he added, "Oh, Lord, please let Arthur come again soon. I thank you for sending him today."

At the same time, Arthur was telling his mother about David, and they had a long talk, which I am sure David would have liked to hear, and which he did hear from Arthur very soon afterward.

The room in which Arthur and his mother talked that evening was very different from the one in which we left

David and Aunt Jane sitting, and yet perhaps there was no more happiness in one than in the other. One had heavy wooden chairs, the other had softly cushioned sofas and divans; one had coarse muslin curtains, the other had draperies of rich lace; one had a Bible and David's Reader, the other had shelves and shelves of books. But God was in each of them, and where He is, nothing else matters.

"Mother," said Arthur, after he had told her about his visit in the afternoon, "I wish papa could cure David. He's such a nice boy! He's the nicest boy I know."

"You seem to be very sure of him."

"Well, you know yourself, sometimes you get 'quainted right away. He likes to play stories, and so do I. He has a king-name too."

"You can go to see him and talk about it all."

"But he can't play it. He says he ought to be strong to play King David. He can't play tournament, either. He wants to be strong so badly!"

"He is stronger than you are."

"Why, mamma!"

"He can keep still patiently, and that is being strong."

"How, mamma?"

"Is it harder to keep still, or to jump and run?"

"To keep still."

"Well, if David does that without murmuring, he is stronger than you. You are always fretful when I want you to try to be quiet for awhile. You will have to learn to control yourself before you can be strong."

"I see, mamma; I forgot that was being strong. But then, he can't play knight."

"Yes, he can."

"Oh, mamma, how?" and Arthur jumped up, eager to hear.

HE TOLD AUNT JANE ABOUT HIS VISITOR.

CHAPTER IV.

King Arthur and Sir Galahad.

o you remember about Sir Galahad?"

"He was one of King Arthur's knights," said Mrs. Bryan in answer to Arthur's question.

"I can't think of anything about him," said Arthur.

Mrs. Bryan remembered something she had read long ago. "There is a poem about him in which he says:

'My strength is as the strength of ten,
Because my heart is pure.'

He cared less for fighting than for being kind and good and true."

"Please say the poetry again, mamma. I want to learn it for David."

Mrs. Bryan repeated it, and Arthur said it after her. Then she asked, "Don't you remember about the Holy Grail?"

"Oh, yes, mamma; it always went with him, didn't it? And all the other knights once left their tournaments to go looking for it."

"Yes, and it can always go with you and with David. You see, they thought they were looking for the cup out of which Christ drank at the Last Supper. But what it really meant, and what they really wanted, was the presence of Christ, their King. You can have your King with you always."

"I wish you would tell David about it."

"You can tell him, dear. Perhaps he may understand you better."

"I'll tell him he can be Sir Galahad."

"Yes, dear. If he keeps near to the King, his heart will be kept pure, and that will give him the greatest strength."

Dr. Bryan's arrival interrupted that

part of the conversation, but Arthur soon led it back to the subject of his new friend.

"Papa, can't you cure David?" he asked wistfully.

"My dear boy, I cannot see why it is that he is not cured. I expected him to be well long before this. If he were a weak, cowardly boy, I should say he did not exert his will; but he seems to be a strong-willed boy. It must be that he needs fresh air and better food. After all, it is a wonder children even live in a place like Shop Row."

Mrs. Bryan looked up from her work, and said with interest, "Couldn't we do anything to help him?"

"Mamma, he could go driving with us!" Arthur exclaimed. "He can walk a little; he could get to the carriage."

"I was thinking of that," replied Mrs. Bryan.

The very next day Arthur hurried over to Shop Row after school. He carried with him the book about King Arthur's court, and as soon as he burst into the room, he exclaimed, "You can be a knight! Mamma says so! And we're coming to take you driving tomorrow!"

It all had to be explained, and Arthur did it very well, on the whole. He fumbled in his pocket for the paper on which he had carefully written the lines about Sir Galahad, and he read them to David very slowly:

"My strength is as the strength of ten,
Because my heart is pure."

David eagerly took the paper from him, and asked, "Who said that?"

"It was Sir Galahad," Arthur replied. "Mamma says he cared for being kind and good and true more than he cared about fighting. She says you can fight battles inside of you — you know how."

"Yes," David said appreciatively.

Arthur continued, "She says you are stronger than I am, because you can keep patient, although you can't run and jump like some boys."

"Is that being strong?"

"She said it took more strength to be patient and still. Once when I wanted to fight with a boy at school, she found out about it and didn't want me to. I said if I didn't fight, the boy would think I was a coward. She asked if it would be harder to fight or not to fight, and of course I thought it would be harder not to fight. She said it was braver to do the hard thing."

"Did you fight him?"

"Yes, and we rolled down the hill into the brook. We both had to stay in all day 'cause we got wet. It was Saturday we did it. He took a cold and was sick a long while. I felt mean all the time—he's a month younger than I am, you know, and that made me feel meaner, too."

David sympathized about the inglorious[7] battle, and Arthur said, "Mamma gave me this ribbon after that, to help me remember to be a Christian knight. She said a Christian knight would try harder to fight his own temper than to fight other boys. I almost

---

[7] Shameful; disgraceful; dishonorable.

forgot — she sent you a ribbon, too. It's in my other pocket."

The ribbon was produced and pinned on David's coat, to his great satisfaction. When Arthur departed some time afterward, his last words were, "We'll call for you tomorrow when we go out driving, if it's a clear day — I forgot mamma said that."

The next day was not clear, however. It was a tantalizing[8] day. It rained awhile, and then stopped so suddenly that you were sure the sun would soon be shining. Then it rained again, but you hoped it would clear by afternoon. But the afternoon was rainier than the morning, and David had to give up the thought of going out.

It would have been the first drive he had ever had, and the first time he had been away from Shop Row since the sad thing happened. Neither you nor I can think what a disappointment it was. The tears crowded into his eyes, but a knight must not cry, he remembered;

---

[8] Tormented by the thought of something hoped for, but out of reach.

so he brushed them all away and took up his slate to add one more item to his list. This time he copied the lines from Arthur's paper, and wrote under them:

It is strong to keep still
when you want to run, if you
keep still pashently.

The night before, when he had told Aunt Jane about how he was going to try to be a knight, she had quoted, "He that is slow to anger is better than the mighty, and he that ruleth his spirit, than he that taketh a city."[9] She had found him the place in Proverbs where it was written, so he thought he would put that down, too. He couldn't find it himself or remember the exact words, but he wrote:

It is stronger not to get
angry than to take a city if
you are a king and can fight.

It is a good thing he had written that

[9] Proverbs 16:32

before Tom Black came toddling in. Tom was a very troublesome three-year-old urchin.[10] He wanted to investigate everything, and his investigations usually led to something serious. This afternoon he wanted David's slate, and nothing else would suit him. David tried to amuse him, and quickly put the slate away, thinking Tom would soon forget about it. Though he seemed to at first, he really had not given up, and at the first opportunity he reached for it, and sent it flying to the floor, where it smashed into a dozen pieces.

"It was only a slate," you say. You break yours often, perhaps. But David had no money to buy another, and Aunt Jane had no money for anything but food and clothes, the plainest of both. It was a very precious slate, because it had been David's constant companion. Besides, it had the records of his life on one side of it.

What poet or statesman would not resent seeing the first chapters of his

---

[10] A small, mischievous boy.

memoirs destroyed before his eyes? Was it easier for David? I am afraid he was very angry. He did not often fly into a passion—it took quite a big cause to make him—but if there was a reason big enough, he could be very angry; and now he had sufficient reason. He was going to push Tom away from his chair and say all the ugly things he could, but the bow of ribbon fell off as he was twisting around. It floated right down to the very piece of slate which held the words, "stronger not to get angry." David saw them and paused. He felt sure his Elder Brother was helping him at that very moment. Instead of pushing Tom away, he said, "Never mind, Tom. You didn't mean to do it; don't cry."

It was a real victory, and our little knight felt that it was, and that his King was glad about it.

CHAPTER V.

"Things I Am Learning."

t may seem strange, but it really happened that the very same afternoon Miss Miller, the village teacher, called as she passed. Something had made her remember the little lame boy for whom Alice Black had once asked for a slate and book, and she thought she would see how he was progressing. She brought some half-filled copybooks[11] with her, and some lead pencils, another Reader, and an old arithmetic.[12] She promised to come and help him herself

---

[11] Books containing models of penmanship.

[12] A book on arithmetic, the most elementary branch of mathematics.

sometimes.

When she had gone away David thought, "Suppose I had been angry with Tom about that slate. Wouldn't I have felt mean when I found out God was going to send me all these things?"

He selected one of the copybooks titled *Things I Am Learning*, and he began to write them again, spelling correctly this time, because the words he wanted were in the new book.

It was several days before he could take the drive, but he was so busy with writing that he never had time to wish for it. When at last the carriage called for him one afternoon, and Mrs. Bryan, Arthur, and he went rolling along by woods and fields, his delight knew no bounds. The first breath of air from the hilltops seemed to give him strength. It was a real pleasure to watch him. His blue eyes sparkled, and his delicately molded cheek glowed, until Mrs. Bryan found herself wondering how the little village boy came by his inheritance of beauty and good manners.

She knew that Aunt Jane was a lady, a princess of the kingdom of God, and that she had taught the little boy confided to her care to be Christ-like in little things. That made him a gentleman, even if he knew nothing of rules of etiquette.

"There are chestnut trees in there," Arthur said, as they passed another grove. "Uncle John and I came there last fall, and we got lots of nuts.

"That's the pond where we skated last winter," he continued as they passed a large sheet of water. "I believe there isn't anything that's as much fun as skating."

"Mike used to skate at nights sometimes. Once he fell in, and it made his mother afraid, so he didn't go any more," David said, to show that he was interested in skating.

"There's a brook on the hillside above that pond, and you can go wading there. We do it every summer," Arthur explained, pointing out the place.

Arthur told about all the good times he had enjoyed here and in the places where he went for his summer outings, and Mrs. Bryan could see that there was not a trace of envy in the heart of the boy who had no such good times. He was pleased at Arthur's pleasure, as if it were his own.

She was ashamed that she had almost been afraid that it might not be good for her son to have a Shop Row boy for a special friend. She had no fears about it now. Today she was pleasing them by calling one King Arthur and the other Sir Galahad, and when they neared the little village again, she said, "Sir Galahad must ride through his parks again soon."

"My parks?" asked David.

"Yes, yours and mine, and everybody's who wants them. They are God's hills and fields, but He lends them to us. The way to have them is to enjoy them."

A year rolled by, and another and another. During that time David took many drives and spent many a day with Arthur. Little by little, he had grown stronger—how he scarcely knew—until he could walk as far as the village school. Dr. Bryan's idea was the right one; all he needed was more bracing[13] air and better food. He received both through the doctor's kindness, and although he was never likely to be as strong as he once had wished, and would still walk with a limp, yet he was no longer helpless.

He still wore the little ribbon—not the same piece, for Mrs. Bryan had renewed both his and Arthur's many times. He had new kinds of battles to fight at school. For instance, one day, when he was very anxious to keep at the head of his class, he could not remember the name of the capital of Virginia when the question came to him. Miss Miller was giving him a little time to reflect, feeling sure he must know it, when a little boy behind him who was saying "Richmond! Richmond!" softly to himself, suddenly whispered it distinctly enough for David to hear. David said it immediately, and kept his place; but all his pleasure had

---

[13] Invigorating; strengthening; stimulating.

gone. He thought he would tell that he had been prompted. Then he reassured himself with the idea that he would have recalled the name himself in a minute; it must have been just coming to him when he heard it. But it had not come. He was cheating—he who had despised other boys for that!

He wanted very much to be number one that day, for it was Friday, and Miss Miller gave a card to any one who remained at the head all week. This would have been his second week, and Aunt Jane would have been so proud! But would she be proud if he cheated? No, indeed! This battle went on all day, and at the last hour, the Sir Galahad part of him conquered. An honor that his King could not bless would not be much ornament to a knight.

Just as Miss Miller was about to give him the card, he said, "Alice Black ought to be number one today; I heard somebody say 'Richmond' while you were waiting for me to remember."

It took only a minute to say it, but it

"ALICE BLACK OUGHT TO BE NUMBER ONE TODAY."

made a different person of him. Instead of feeling like a coward, he felt he had the strength of ten, because his heart was pure.

CHAPTER VI.

An Unexpected Comfort.

here was in David's school one little girl whose brothers always made her carry their books home. They would run off to the woods themselves, leaving her to trudge along with her burden the best way she could. The first time David noticed it, he hurried up to Ella and said, "Let me have the books. I'll walk home your way today."

She looked very grateful at first, but in a minute she exclaimed, "Oh, no! It would tire you. You are not strong."

It always saddened David a little to be reminded of that, but he said brightly, "Well, I'll carry part of them. We'll divide them evenly, so that neither of us will be tired."

Every day he walked home with Ella Knox. Her brothers laughed, of course, and began to make fun of him. He could not play many boy games and was often with the girls at recess, so this gave occasion for more joking, which nearly made him angry at first. He swallowed the anger all down, however, and went along with a smiling face, until at last the boys themselves began to have a feeling that there was strength in his silent cheerfulness that was not to be despised.

David soon became a leader in his way. Disputes were settled by appealing to his authority, and his wisdom was renowned.

The records headed *Things I Am Learning* covered several pages now. These are some of his later paragraphs:

God sends people to you just when you need them.

Our King helps you to do
what He wants you to do.
Other kings only command.
It does not matter what
other people say if you can
hear the King saying inside
of you that you did right.

One day he found an unexpected comfort. It was in Mr. Stanton's Sunday-school class, for there was a Sunday-school at Alverton, although there was no church and no minister. The lesson was about the man born blind,[14] and when the boys had expressed great sympathy for him, Mr. Stanton said, "I should be glad to have been that man."

Every boy looked astonished except David, who eagerly awaited the explanation.

Mr. Stanton continued. "Christ used him. He needed somebody to be born blind so that He could make him to see, to teach the people that He was the Light of the world."

[14] John 9:1-41

The next day David wrote in his chronicles:

> Maybe Christ needed somebody to be lame here. I ought to be glad if He wants to use me.

But he could not help longing to be able to aid Aunt Jane. She did not seem well, and if he were only strong he might get a place in the factory now, for there were boys there no older than he. He thought about it and thought about it, and at last there came a time when it seemed as if his wish might be realized.

Every summer a girl was hired to make sample-cards of the goods manufactured in the Alverton Mills. It was very easy work, and Martha Flint had been doing it for the last three years when she came to spend her vacation with her family. She stayed in the city with her uncle the rest of the year so that she could go to school there, and the little she earned in the summer was a great help to her. Indeed, if it had not been for that, she would not have been able to go to school, for it bought her clothes for the whole year, and she managed to have very few other expenses.

This year when David was so anxious about Aunt Jane, he heard that they needed a sample-card maker earlier than usual, and there would be extra work all summer. He told Arthur about it, and one day the two hurried to the superintendent to apply for the position for David.

"You are too young," Mr. Colton said gruffly.

"But I could do the work," David assured him. "I watched Martha do it last year."

"A boy is never neat enough. We've had no success with boys."

"But David is neat," Arthur interposed. "He learned to do girl-things when he was in the house so long. He can sew on buttons and mend his clothes."

"Boys always mix up the samples."

"YOU ARE TOO YOUNG," MR. COLTON SAID GRUFFLY.

"I would be very careful," David said.

He did look like a neat, careful boy, Mr. Colton thought. At last he said, "I'll let you try. You can go at once to the room. The man there will tell you what to do."

So David was installed as a "hand." How he enjoyed his work! At the end of the first week he persuaded Aunt Jane to take a little vacation, assuring her that by living carefully they could make his wages suffice for awhile.

The sample-cards were never made more neatly, and he even learned the names of the styles of flannel so that he could label them himself. When Martha came, she was surprised to find a little boy at her work; but she cheerfully joined with him, and found him quite an interesting companion when they had time to talk.

"What makes you so careful about the back?" she asked one day. "Mr. Colton never looks at the back of a card; he is in too big a hurry when he sends them away."

"But I want it all to be good," David replied.

"Why?" persisted Martha.

"Because — because," David faltered, "because God sees it all."

"Oh! Do you suppose He cares?"

"Yes; there's something in the Bible about doing everything as unto Him."[15]

After that, Martha often asked David questions merely to make him talk. She liked to ridicule people; she seemed to see all the queer ways of the country folks.

"Did you ever see anybody look so funny as Jim Healey?" she would ask. "That hat must have belonged to his great-grandfather, and he always has it pressed down over his eyes."

"But he can't afford to buy a new one," David would answer; "his wife is sick all the time, and he spends all his money for her. I think his eyes are weak, and that makes him push his hat down.

---

[15] Colossians 3:23

Once mine hurt, and I had to wear my hat that way."

"You never see anything funny."

"Yes I do."

And she knew he did, for they often laughed heartily together. She was glad he did not make fun of everything, after all; for he would very likely have teased her about her red hair as her brothers did.

One day he came with a new piece of ribbon on his coat.

"Where's the old one?" she asked. She knew about the meaning of it by this time.

"In my pocket," said David.

"Will you give it to me?'

"I'll give you the new one, and wear the other myself. It wasn't very dirty, but Arthur's going to the city, so his mother gave him a new one, and we always change them together."

"Can a girl be one of your knights?"

"I don't know; I reckon she can. Why, you would be a lady—the Lady Martha."

"What do I have to do?"

"Whatever the King tells you. You will know."

"But I don't belong to Him."

"You can belong to Him. You only need to ask Him to make your heart pure and clean. Only then can you fight the battles of the King — those great and fierce battles inside of us."

"Oh, I do want to belong to the King!" exclaimed Martha.

David smiled.

"I have been ashamed of myself lately — ever since the time about the back of the cards."

"It's alright, Martha. We serve a merciful King. I am so glad you want to be a Christian!"

CHAPTER VII.

A Very Brief Struggle.

he weeks flew by and they were happy weeks, for David had found a friend. Martha had been a friend before, but he never found any real pleasure in his friendships unless their bond was service of the King. And now Martha loved his King.

One morning she came in with tears in her eyes, and when David asked what was the matter, she replied, "Mr. Colton says he will not need me after today. There will only be work enough for one, and, as you will be a regular hand, you ought to have it."

A very brief struggle went on in

David's heart. He thought of Aunt Jane and her much-needed rest, and he thought of Martha and her cherished hopes of going to the public school in the city awhile longer. Aunt Jane would not want him to take Martha's place. Sir Galahad would not do it. The King's Word said something about "in honor preferring one another."[16]

"You must not go," he said quickly. "I only came because you were not home yet."

"Did you really mean only to do it for awhile?"

"Of course; I knew it was your place."

"But Mr. Colton would rather have you, David."

"Not when he knows I only came to work until you could do it yourself."

He immediately went to Mr. Colton and explained. The superintendent was greatly surprised, but was willing to keep Martha, if David desired it.

"Let me see," he said thoughtfully, "I

---

[16] Romans 12:10

wonder if you could do some copying for me. Write your name on that paper." David wrote boldly:

David Kerry Grandon.

"Your hand is quite plain. I suppose you could copy these bills for me. The bookkeeper is taking his vacation, and they are piling up too rapidly."

The copying afforded several days' work, and the last one that David spent in the office proved an important one, for that was when the glad thing happened.

All that last day in the office, David felt very quiet and a little sad. Whenever he thought of Aunt Jane, he would breathe the prayer, "Lord, help me to know what to do next." He did not know that the next thing for him was very near him even then.

He had reached the last page of bills in the big book when Mr. Kerry, the minister from Elkton, entered the office. He was quite a young man, and had had the church in Elkton for only a few months, so David had never seen him

before. His errand to Mr. Colton was
to ask if he might preach in the hall at
Alverton on Sunday night, once every
two weeks. As soon as he had heard of
the little factory town with no church, he
had felt as if he ought to do something
there; and his own church had consented
to have a prayer-meeting every alternate
Sunday night, so that he could be free
to preach at Alverton. However, the
owners of the place had to be consulted
first through Mr. Colton.

David told him the superintendent
was not in, but he would return soon;
so the Reverend Mr. Kerry sat down to
wait.

Now that very piece of paper on
which David had written his name
several days before lay on the desk,
propped up against an ink-stand, so
that when the minister's eyes wandered
over toward David, they could not help
resting on it. Dozens of other pieces of
paper had been thrown into the waste-
basket during those few days. The only
reason that one escaped was because it

had a mission in the world. It could not be destroyed yet. God was going to use it. Mr. Kerry read:

David Kerry Grandon

and started up involuntarily. The boy at the desk raised his large blue eyes, and it seemed as if they sent an electric shock through the preacher.

"Whose name is that?" he demanded.

"Mine," answered David.

"And part of it is mine, and also my father's. How came you to be called David Kerry?"

"My mother called me after her father."

"Where is your mother?" he asked excitedly.

"She died long ago, when I was very little."

"What was her name?"

"Rose Kerry."

"And your father's?"

"James Grandon."

"Where did she die? In this town? In Shop Row, all alone?"

"No, sir; we lived in the city then, I think. I don't know much about it. Aunt Jane knows."

"Who is she?"

"My father's sister. He brought me to her. He's dead too."

"I see it all," murmured the preacher. "It must have been while we were abroad that she died. And we thought she was hiding from us. My boy, you are my nephew. Your mother was my sister. When may I see your aunt?"

David was speechless. Could it be that he was related to this fine-looking young man?

"You look just like your mother," Mr. Kerry said.

"Aunt Jane says I do," David managed to answer.

"Do you remember her?"

"No, sir; I was too little when she died."

"When may I see your aunt?"

"She is in the weave-room now. She came back to her work today."

Mr. Kerry ran into Mr. Colton at the

door, and stopped long enough to ask permission to see Jane Grandon. In a few minutes, in the noise of the looms, he was listening to the story of David's mother.

"She loved Jim," Aunt Jane repeated every little while.

At last Mr. Kerry said, "I know she did. We did not want her to marry him, but we never meant to lose sight of her. We went to Europe after she was married. There was an estate in Scotland to be settled, and some of it belonged to us. We were there two years, and never heard from her in that time. When we came home, we could find no trace of her."

"The boy has been such a comfort to me!" Aunt Jane said in a choking voice. She felt sure they would want to take him from her now.

Mr. Kerry left her without saying another word. He took David with him when he departed from the office, and he forgot all about his errand that time.

"You must come home with me," he

said to the boy.

"But Aunt Jane will want to talk to me when she comes."

"Then I'll stay here until then."

It took them a very little while to become acquainted. David told him all about the years when he could not walk, about Arthur, about Sir Galahad, about the work at the factory. He even let him see the precious book of *Things I Am Learning*.

"You must tell me how you learned every one of them," his Uncle David said.

"Oh, that would take a long while! It does not take long to write them down, but it often took a long while to find them out."

"I have taken longer than you to find them out."

"I thought you knew them all. You are a preacher."

"Yes, I am a preacher, and that reminds me—I came here to ask if I could preach at Alverton. I must go back and ask Mr. Colton."

CHAPTER VIII.

"BRING HIM AT ONCE!"

r. Colton's permission for the preaching would have been readily obtained, but he had to consult his employers; so he could not give Mr. Kerry an answer for a few days. In factory towns like Alverton, the man who owns the mills, houses, store, and every foot of ground, is king in a small way. Alverton was owned by a family-run company in which the oldest member of the family had the final authority.

The minister returned in company with Aunt Jane this time. "My father will want to see David," he was saying. "I must come back for him tomorrow, after I have broken the news to his grandfather."

"And his grandmother?" inquired Aunt Jane.

"She has been at rest many years, Miss Grandon. My father and I are alone. Our old servant is our housekeeper at the parsonage in Elkton."

"Are you going to take David from me?"

"His grandfather will desire it, I am sure," answered the minister. And that was all.

Two people did not sleep much the night after that eventful day — Aunt Jane, who felt that she was giving up her boy; and the old man in the parsonage at Elkton, who was grieving for his daughter, while he rejoiced at finding her son.

"Bring him to me at once," he had ordered, but his son assured him that he had better wait until the next day to let David have time to get over his bewilderment.

The next morning the man insisted on

having him come immediately. "He must not stay an hour longer in that place. How do I know what he is learning?" he said fiercely.

"But father, he has spent all his life there. A few more hours cannot change him."

"Well, bring him — bring him at once!"

So Mr. Kerry appeared in Shop Row at an early hour, and David was soon on his way to Elkton.

"You had better take all you will want with you; your grandfather will not let you come back," Mr. Kerry told David.

Not come back! David was startled. To leave Aunt Jane, because he had found an uncle!

"But Aunt Jane will want me!" he stammered.

"You belong to your grandfather, first of all."

"But Aunt Jane took care of me always. I've been belonging more and more to her all the time. I want to work for her again."

"BUT AUNT JANE WILL WANT ME," DAVID STAMMERED.

The Reverend David Kerry was silenced. It was useless to argue with the clear-eyed boy. Perhaps his grandfather would have more success with him.

When David was ushered into the elder Mr. Kerry's presence, he was a little afraid of the stern-looking man who grasped him by the shoulders and said, "Rose's eyes! My poor little Rose!" Afterward, when the pain of the first meeting was over and the old man smiled, David saw tenderness behind the sternness, so he was no longer afraid.

There was so much he must tell that the hours passed very rapidly before the noonday meal, and more rapidly still after. Mr. Kerry took a nap in the afternoon, and David and his uncle strolled around the garden together.

"What shall I preach about at Alverton?" asked the latter.

"Oh, preach what boys will like!"

"Boys do not like sermons, do they?"

"Yes, they do, if they can understand them. I mean I think they do. I have only heard a few sermons. We only have prayer-meetings at Alverton."

"Did you ever come to church at Elkton?"

"Yes, a few times with Arthur, but we never seem to belong there, you know."

"Why?"

"We didn't know any people."

"But you will soon know the people now." Then the young minister stopped suddenly in his walk, and exclaimed, "I have an idea! Let me have your book of the things you have learned. I'll take my subjects from it."

"Would it be any good?"

"Yes, it would."

They walked a little while longer, until David remembered how late it was. "Oh, I must go home!" he said. "Aunt Jane will expect me to be there by the time she is out of the factory."

"You had better see your grandfather. There he is on the porch now."

They went toward the porch together, and David said, "I came to say good-by. I've had a lovely time."

"What do you mean?" asked his

grandfather. "You are to stay with us now."

"But Aunt Jane will want me."

"She knows you belong to me."

"Yes, and she would let me stay, but I know I ought to belong to her."

"I want to send you to the Academy here, and afterward to the University."

Little Sir Galahad was sorely tempted then. But would it be knightly to leave Aunt Jane, when he had intended to take care of her in her old age?

"You shall stay!" said the old man determinedly; and his son wondered how the boy dared resist him.

The boy was strong in spirit. Nearly all the twelve years of his life he had been striving for that strength. He never appeared to have to wait long to hear his King's command, and the power seemed to come with the order.

"It would not be right for me to leave Aunt Jane," he said gently, but very firmly.

The old man could not stand the frank, truthful gaze of the blue eyes. His own eyes dropped, and at last he said submissively, "Let him go this evening. We shall see about it later."

David hurried back to Shop Row and the little low room, as if he were afraid of what he had left behind him at Elkton. It had been a sore temptation, but his grandfather knew nothing about it. He was half afraid the boy could not appreciate the advantages he offered him, and did not know how much David longed for books and culture and all that would be denied him if he lived at Alverton. I think David never even knew he wanted them until they came so near him, but now he saw very clearly what he was giving up.

Aunt Jane asked very few questions that night. She did not intend to approach the subject of the separation until it was forced upon her. She thought perhaps Mr. Kerry was giving her a few days to get used to the thought. But the next day, when she was summoned from the factory at ten o'clock in the morning, she was sure her hour of trial had come.

A carriage stood before the poor little house in Shop Row. In the room she found David's grandfather and his uncle.

"Oh, Aunt Jane, my grandfather has come to see you!" David cried out, and she wondered how he could be so joyful.

Mr. Kerry, the elder, studied Aunt Jane's honest, good face for a few minutes. Then he said slowly, "Your boy refuses to be separated from you, Miss Grandon. We have come to the conclusion that he needs you, and we need you. Will you accept the position of housekeeper in our home? Our old cook is growing careless, but under your supervision I think the house might be easily managed. Will you come to us?"

CHAPTER IX.

The First Sermon.

unt Jane went to the parsonage when David left. During the first busy days there everybody forgot about the preaching at Alverton on Sunday nights, but one morning a letter came from Mr. Colton to say that the chief member of the firm objected to the new plan.

David was sorely disappointed, and so were they all. Arthur, who had to come down the other side of the hill to see David now, was even wrathful.

"Grumpy old czar!"[17] he said. "He

---

[17] An emperor or king, or a man of great authority or power.

must think the people are like his old machines. I am going to ask papa to go and see him."

It was Mrs. Bryan who thought of the best plan. She had heard that Mr. Kerry intended to preach from the subjects in David's book, and that he had already been finding texts for the sermons. "Let David go to see Mr. Mayberry," she said. "He can take his book with him and show Mr. Mayberry what the sermons will be about. That may convince him there will be no harm in them."

One bright morning the minister and his nephew took the train for the city. They went to Mr. Mayberry's mansion together, but only the boy was ushered into the library to see the gentleman.

"I am David Grandon," he explained. "My uncle is the Reverend David Kerry, the man who wants to preach at Alverton. He sent me to tell you what he wants to preach about."

"I don't want any preaching there!" growled the agitated man.

But David was not afraid. He felt sure

the King wanted him to succeed.

"You know the people cannot hear any preaching unless they go all the way to Elkton, and it makes you too tired when you have worked all the week," he said.

"What do you know about it?"

"I have lived there until just now. I have worked some, too."

The old man was amused. The boy was interesting. "What did you do?" he asked.

"I made sample-cards."

"It's a wonder your uncle would let you associate with the heathen in that town."

"I was a 'heathen,' too. He didn't know me then. As soon as he found me, he took me to Elkton."

"Now you want to be a missionary, do you?"

"I want Uncle David to preach to the boys—the boys only as old as I am."

"How old is that?"

"Twelve, sir."

"Well, what do you want him to preach?"

"I didn't want to tell him what to preach, but you see, I was lame for a long while—more than I am now. I couldn't walk at all. I used to write down the things I learned, and when Uncle David saw the book, he said he could find subjects out of that."

"Is that the book you have there?"

"Yes, sir."

"Let me see it."

That was more amusing than the boy at first, but in a few minutes the old man ceased smiling.

"Where did you get all this?" he asked.

"I learned it."

"Do many boys at Alverton learn these things?"

"I don't know; they don't have time to write them down."

"So you think I ought to let your uncle preach."

"Yes, sir."

"You must leave me this list of

subjects, and after I have considered them I will send you my answer. Will that be satisfactory?"

"Yes, sir. Thank you for letting me come to see you. Good-by, sir." David was just leaving the room when Mr. Mayberry called him back.

"Tell him he can preach. I'll keep the book until I look over it. I'll send it out to you."

David was radiant when he reached his uncle in the big parlor. "He says you can preach! He says you can preach!"

All the way home they talked and planned about it. The text of the first sermon was to be "Learn of Me," because David's first sentence was, "God wants me to learn about Him."

"How shall I tell them to learn about Him?" Mr. Kerry asked.

"Tell them to look out for the things He does for them."

Then David recalled how he met Arthur when the dog chased the cat, and how the books came after his slate was broken. He recalled how he learned to

write neatly because of his lameness —
which allowed him to work at the
factory.

Uncle David smiled. "I have an idea.
After the Sunday sermon we will offer
blue ribbons to anyone who wants to
learn the lessons of Sir Galahad and fight
the battles from within."

The sermon was a success. David
and Arthur wore their blue ribbons
proudly. Lady Martha wore her ribbon
too, and the three stood in the front of
the crowded room. Many came forward
that day; some to receive their ribbon
and some to receive their King. Even
Mr. Mayberry came to observe the
proceedings, and some said that he left
with a tear in his eye.

Over the course of the year, there
were many changes in Alverton. Folks
became kinder, employees worked
harder, Mr. Colton became more thankful
and generous, and Sir Galahad was the
talk of the town for many years to come.

David did attend school at Elkton
with Arthur. His lameness was mostly

cured; only when he was tired did he notice it.

Aunt Jane enjoyed the housekeeping very much after the years of harder toil in the factory. She kept close watch of David, and whenever he seemed inclined to be exultant about his returning strength, she reminded him of the greater strength which the years of lameness had taught him.

Sir Galahad grew up to be a strong and mighty knight of the King of kings, for "his strength was as the strength of ten, because his heart was pure."

THE END.

"Blessed are the pure in heart,
For they shall see God."
MATTHEW 5:8

Books by A.L.O.E.

The Battle (Sequel to *The Giant Killer*)

Dashed to Pieces

Escape from the Eagle's Nest

Exiles in Babylon *(Heroes of Faith Series)*

The Giant Killer

The Golden Fleece

The Haunted Room

Hebrew Heroes

The Jewel

Ned Franks: The One-Armed Sailor

The Passage

The Pilgrim's Call

Pride and His Prisoners

Rescued from Egypt *(Heroes of Faith Series)*

The Robbers' Cave

The Shepherd of Bethlehem *(Heroes of Faith Series)*

Triumph over Midian *(Heroes of Faith Series)*

The Wanderer in Africa

A.L.O.E. (1821-1893) was born Charlotte Maria Tucker near Barnet, Middlesex, England. She was the sixth child of her parents and was educated at home. Under the pseudonym A.L.O.E. (A Lady of England), she wrote over 140 books for children, most with an obvious moral, and devoted the proceeds to charity. In 1875, she left England for India and spent the rest of her life there, engaged in missionary work.

WWW.LAMPLIGHTER.NET

BOOKS BY
CHRISTOPH VON SCHMID

THE BASKET OF FLOWERS

THE BIRD'S NEST

THE CAPTIVE

FIRE IN THE SKY

THE INHERITANCE

THE LITTLE LAMB

THE LOST RUBY

THE PAINTED FLY AND OTHER STORIES

ROSA OF LINDEN CASTLE

SCHMID'S TALES

THE WHITE DOVE

WORTH MORE THAN GOLD

CHRISTOPH VON SCHMID (1768-1854) was born in Bavaria, studied theology, and became an ordained priest in 1791. In 1796 he was placed at the head of a large school, where he began writing stories for children, reading them after school hours as a reward, on condition that the children would write the stories down at home. In 1841, he published a complete edition of his scattered writings in 24 volumes. He is considered the pioneer writer of books for children, and his stories have been translated into at least 24 languages.

1-888-A-GOSPEL • 1-888-246-7735

BOOKS BY
MRS. O.F. WALTON

CHRISTIE, THE KING'S SERVANT

CHRISTIE'S OLD ORGAN

LITTLE FAITH

THE LOST CLUE

MY MATES AND I

A PEEP BEHIND THE SCENES

SAVED AT SEA

THROW ME OVERBOARD

WHEN YOU LEAST EXPECT IT

WINTER'S FOLLY

MRS. O.F. WALTON (1849-1939) was born Amy Catherine Deck in Kent, England. Shortly after her marriage to Octavius Frank Walton, the couple moved to Jerusalem, where Octavius ministered in a church on Mount Zion and Amy wrote *A Peep Behind the Scenes*. Her book *Christie's Old Organ* was one of the earliest books in history of both Christian and children's literature to be translated and published in Japan.

WWW.LAMPLIGHTER.NET

Books by Amy Le Feuvre

Amy Le Feuvre (1861-1929) was born in London, England, and grew up in a large family. She was a prolific author of children's books with a strong Christian message. Her book *Teddy's Button* was one of the most popular of all late Victorian children's stories.

WWW.LAMPLIGHTER.NET

Books of the Year

*Books of the Year are determined by biblical insights,
captivating plots, and life-changing character lessons.*

- 2018 – The Treasure of the Secret Cove
  – The Secret Bridge
- 2017 – Launch the Lifeboat
  – Escape from the Eagle's Nest
- 2016 – A 'Strordinary Little Maid
  – The Locked Cupboard
- 2015 – Joseph's Shield
  – The Haunted Room
- 2014 – Frozen Fire
  – Comfortable Troubles
- 2013 – It's All Real True
  – The King's Gold
- 2012 – Jack the Conqueror
  – Falsely Accused
- 2011 – Wälty and the Great Geyer
  – True to the Last
- 2010 – The Wanderer in Africa
  – The White Gypsy
- 2009 – Sir Malcolm and the Missing Prince
  – Exiles in Babylon
- 2008 – My Mates and I
  – The Shepherd of Bethlehem
- 2007 – The Lost Clue
- 2006 – Ishmael
- 2005 – The Giant Killer
  – The Hidden Hand
- 2004 – The Cross Triumphant
- 2003 – Sir Knight of the Splendid Way
- 2002 – Shipwrecked, But Not Lost
- 2001 – Teddy's Button
- 2000 – The Hedge of Thorns
- 1999 – The Lamplighter
- 1998 – A Peep Behind the Scenes
- 1997 – Titus: A Comrade of the Cross
- 1996 – The Basket of Flowers

1-888-A-GOSPEL • 1-888-246-7735

ILLUSTRATED BOOKS

We are delighted to present to you this creative collection with beautiful illustrations for young visual learners. Reinforce character building and stimulate imagination with our Illustrated Collection. To view the complete collection, visit www.lamplighter.net.

TRUSTY: TRIED AND TRUE
Written by Mark Hamby, *Really* written by Debbie Hamby
Illustrated by Jennifer Brandon

This adorable adventure is bursting with colorful imagery to heighten a child's imagination and stir creativity. Learn about selfishness, pride, and vanity through the characters of Brawny, Smarty, and Beauty, and be inspired by our hero Trusty, who courageously tries to help. This will surely become a family favorite to be read over and over again!

TEDDY'S BUTTON, ILLUSTRATED
Rewritten by Mark Hamby

Join Teddy in his mischievous adventures as he discovers that you don't win the battle with guns and hate, you win the battle with love, and your greatest enemy is yourself. You will never forget what happens when Teddy enlists in the Lord's army!

THE THREE WEAVERS, ILLUSTRATED
Rewritten by Mark Hamby
Illustrated by Jennifer Brandon

A delightful allegory for fathers to read with their daughters—not just once, but over and over again. This illustrated rendition reveals how each weaver prepares his daughter to weave a mantle perfectly suited for the prince. But each father uses a different approach, and the consequences

are very revealing! Enjoy many thought-provoking conversations, creating memories for years to come.

Lamplighter Theatre

Lamplighter Theatre helps to fulfill the mission of Lamplighter by bringing redemptive hope to the world through dramatic audio. Forged through the commitment and sacrifice of a dedicated team, Lamplighter Theatre now airs on 1800 radio stations in 29 countries. With the talent of world-renowned actors, writers, directors, music composers, and sound engineers, Lamplighter Theatre creatively brings redemptive hope to broken lives, and compels its listeners to live life skillfully and sacrificially for the benefit of others.

Sir Malcolm and the Missing Prince
2-Disc Audio Drama

Inside the castle walls a battle rages in the heart of a widowed king. His son, the young Prince Hubert, has proven himself to be an unworthy heir to the throne. But a bold intervention by the king's most trusted knight could prove to be the cure. In the remote lands of this vast kingdom, far from the walls of the palace, Hugh will learn that the requirement of kingship is servanthood. *Best for ages 6-11.*

Approximate Time: 2 hrs.

Frozen Fire
2-Disc Audio Drama

The events that lead up to Betty's pivotal decision demonstrate the true meaning of humility, servanthood, and love. Inspired by a true story, Betty must come face to face with a dreaded foe. Facing myriad trials, including abandonment and the death-

grip of a terrifying blizzard, her love for her devoted servant trumps all. You will fall in love with Betty, whose loyalty is demonstrated through tremendous courage and sacrifice. *Frozen Fire* will keep you on the edge of your seat! Great for the entire family.

Approximate Time: 2 hrs.

Learn more, listen to samples, and view entire drama collection at
WWW.LAMPLIGHTER.NET

BEST FOR...

The 'Best For' Collections are designed for those individuals who have seen this engaging collection of books and wondered which would be best for their children. We have selected an array of stories for each age group to give you just a taste of what Lamplighter books are all about.

BEST FOR AGES 6-11

BASIL; OR, HONESTY AND INDUSTRY

CHRISTIE'S OLD ORGAN

THE GIANT KILLER

HELEN'S TEMPER

JACK THE CONQUEROR

JESSICA'S FIRST PRAYER

JILL'S RED BAG

JOSEPH'S SHIELD

LITTLE SIR GALAHAD

LITTLE THREADS

PROBABLE SONS

TEDDY'S BUTTON

THE WHITE DOVE

BEST FOR AGES 9-14

THE BASKET OF FLOWERS

THE CAPTIVE

THE GOLDEN THREAD

THE HEDGE OF THORNS

THE LITTLE LAMB

MY GOLDEN SHIP

HAND ON THE BRIDLE

A PEEP BEHIND THE SCENES

RISING TO THE TOP

THE ROBBERS' CAVE

ROSA OF LINDEN CASTLE

SHIPWRECKED, BUT NOT LOST

THE WHITE KNIGHTS

BEST FOR AGES 12-99

THE ALABASTER BOX

ESCAPE FROM THE EAGLE'S NEST

THE HAUNTED ROOM

THE HIDDEN HAND

ISHMAEL

THE LAMPLIGHTER

THE LOST CLUE

SIR KNIGHT OF THE SPLENDID WAY

THE WHITE GYPSY

WWW.LAMPLIGHTER.NET

myLAMPLIGHTER
BOOK & AUDIO CLUB

The *myLamplighter Book Club* allows you to follow your own personalized strategic plan as you make a wise investment for your family. We are offering you the opportunity to own the entire Lamplighter collection at your own pace, so that you are in control of your investment.

- SIMPLICITY – YOU choose which titles you would like to receive each month.
- SAVINGS – YOU decide how much money you'd like to save each month!
- CONVENIENCE – YOU maintain and update your account anytime, anywhere.

You can switch plans or temporarily put your club on hold.
You can remove titles from your queue.
You can update and maintain your account online.
Shipping is FREE! *Book Club is not offered outside the US.*
Membership is FREE!
Character Comprehension Quizzes are FREE - $199 value!

PLAN 1	**1 Book per month**
PLAN 2	**2 Books per month**
PLAN 3	**3 Books per month**
PLAN 4	**4 Books per month**

Book Club members can add a New Release at any time to any plan at a 15% discount and free shipping.

TO SIGN UP
Log in at www.lamplighter.net/book-audio-club.

1-888-A-GOSPEL • 1-888-246-7735

THE
LAMPLIGHTER MISSION

Printing books of high quality with an emphasis on character development, biblical insights, artistic design, excellence, and skilled craftsmanship is an integral part of the Lamplighter Mission. Guided by our mission "to make ready a people prepared for the Lord" (Luke 1:17), Lamplighter Publishing and Bindery is strategically engaged by building Christlike character one story at a time. Through the mystery and adventure of Lamplighter stories, the framework of character development is formed and the pursuit of excellence is cultivated. The dominant theme of hope is developed by characters who persevere in adversity, being fully convinced that nothing is impossible with God.

It is the Lamplighter commitment that each book instills moral values through role models that either demonstrate exemplary behavior or suffer the consequences of making wrong choices. A riveting plot, a worthy theme, and endearing characters will motivate readers, both young and old, to adopt a similar moral code by emulating the characters that have now been etched into their awakened conscience.

The goal of Lamplighter Ministries is to cultivate a renaissance of creative excellence that inspires one to know God intimately and proclaim Him passionately. At the Lamplighter Guild, students have the opportunity to work alongside world-class actors, scriptwriters, sound designers, music composers, oil painters, theologians, culinary artists, and other master teachers.

Through these masters, Lamplighter Theatre was established, providing a platform from which Lamplighter books are adapted into classic audio dramas now aired in over 30 countries. Lamplighter Ministries stands on the shoulders of those who have built a good foundation. It is our commitment to remain faithful to these high standards and inspire others to do the same and more. In the words of Solomon, "Do you see a man skillful in his work? He will stand before kings; he will not stand before obscure men" (Proverbs 22:29).

For more information about Lamplighter Ministries, visit www.lamplighter.net or www.lamplighterguild.com. To order a free catalog go to www.lamplighter.net or call toll free 1-888-A-GOSPEL (1-888-246-7735).

LAMPLIGHTER *Publishing*

BUILDING CHRISTLIKE CHARACTER ... ONE STORY AT A TIME

A DIVISION OF LAMPLIGHTER MINISTRIES INTERNATIONAL

To request a catalog, please contact us:
Phone: 1-888-A-GOSPEL (1-888-246-7735)
or 1-570-585-1314
Email: *mail@lamplighter.net*
or visit our website at *www.lamplighter.net*.

ISBN 978-1-58474-100-8

51400 >

9 781584 741008